For Mom & Dad
(who taught me how to hug)

A Book of Hugs

by Dave Ross

HarperCollins*Publishers*

Copyright © 1980 by David H. Ross. All rights reserved. Printed in the United States of America.
LC: 79-7896
CIP Data Available
First paperback edition, 1991.
ISBN 0-06-107418-7 (pbk.)

hug (həg), *v*., hugged, hug·ging
—*vt*. 1. To clasp a person or
thing in one's arms; to embrace
[? Scand; cf. Icel *hugga* to soothe,
console; akin to OE *hogian* to
care for] — *n*. an embrace

hugger, *n*., one who hugs
[*see* A]–Ant., huggee [Obs.]
a person or thing that receives
a hug [*see* B]

huggable, adj., possessing
an affectionate nature or
qualities desirable to hug
[*see* fig. 1]–Ant., unhuggable
[*see* fig. 2]

figure 1

figure 2

Animal Hugs
Fish Hugs

Fish hugs are very cold and seldom returned.
P.S. Never hug a shark.

Three kinds of Bear Hugs

(bare!)

Bear hugs are very strong. Be careful not to hurt.

Octopus Hug

An octopus hugs with its whole body.

Porcupine Hug

Porcupine hugs are done very carefully.

Puppy Hugs

Puppy hugs are very soft and wet.

Fraidycat Hugs

Fraidycat hugs make you feel safe.

Piggyback Hug*

* Sometimes called riding piggyback.

A good way to travel or see a parade.

People Hugs
Mommy Hugs

You can never hug a Mommy too much.

Daddy Hug

Daddy hugs are best when he first walks in the door.

Grandpa Hugs

Grandpa hugs are sometimes given while sitting.

Grandma Hugs

Grandma hugs can be found anywhere, but are especially nice in the kitchen.

Brother Hug ✳
✳Usually called a Buddy Hug.

Note:
A circle of buddy huggers is called a huddle.

Sister Hug✳
✳Also known as a Single-Arm Hug.

Single-arm hugs are good for people who walk together (even if they aren't sisters).

BabyHugs

Baby hugs are given with a little tickle.
(Sometimes they can get you a little wet.)

Great Aunt Mary Hug

A Great Aunt Mary hug can be given by
any large lady you see only once a year.
(You will usually end up with lipstick on your cheek.)

ArmHugs

Arm hugs are good for people who are too big for you to get your arms around.

Hand Hugs✳

✳ Usually called holding hands.
Sometimes called shaking hands.

Never hand-hug with dirty hands unless the
other person has dirty hands too.

Knee Hugs

Knee hugs are for tall people.
Warning: Never try to knee-hug a moving person.

Thing Hugs
Blanket Hug

Everyone needs some kind of blanket.

Tree Hugs

Some trees are easier to hug than others.
Note: If you hug a pine tree too long you get stuck on it.

Rock Hugs

BE A LITTLE BOULDER

Rock hugs are very hard on your face.

Pricker Bush Hugs

Never hug a pricker bush. (Or poison ivy or cactus.)

Ice Cube Hug

Ice cube hugs are quite common in February.

Lamppost Hug

A lamppost hug can save you from a painful experience.

Sandwich Hug

The whole family can get into a sandwich hug.

Special Hugs
Birthday Hugs

A birthday hug is a present anyone can afford.

Report Card Hugs

A Hug

Bee Hug

Sea Hug

Hurt Hugs

Hurt hugs make the pain go away.

Winner Hugs

Loser Hugs

Facts & Hints About Hugs

Hug someone at least once a day and
twice on a rainy day.

Hug with a smile; closed eyes are optional.

A snuggle is a longish hug.

Bedtime hugs help chase away bad dreams

Never hug tomorrow someone you could
hug today.